Dear Parent:
Your child's love of reading starts here!

Every child learns to read in a different way and at his or her own speed. Some go back and forth between reading levels and read favorite books again and again. Others read through each level in order. You can help your young reader improve and become more confident by encouraging his or her own interests and abilities. From books your child reads with you to the first books he or she reads alone, there are I Can Read Books for every stage of reading:

SHARED READING
Basic language, word repetition, and whimsical illustrations, ideal for sharing with your emergent reader

BEGINNING READING
Short sentences, familiar words, and simple concepts for children eager to read on their own

READING WITH HELP
Engaging stories, longer sentences, and language play for developing readers

READING ALONE
Complex plots, challenging vocabulary, and high-interest topics for the independent reader

ADVANCED READING
Short paragraphs, chapters, and exciting themes for the perfect bridge to chapter books

I Can Read Books have introduced children to the joy of reading since 1957. Featuring award-winning authors and illustrators and a fabulous cast of beloved characters, I Can Read Books set the standard for beginning readers.

A lifetime of discovery begins with the magical words **"I Can Read!"**

Visit www.icanread.com for information on enriching your child's reading experience.

I Can Read Book® is a trademark of HarperCollins Publishers.

The Berenstain Bears: We Love Baseball! Copyright © 2017 by Berenstain Publishing, Inc. All rights reserved. Manufactured in U.S.A. No part of this book may be used or reproduced in any manner whatsoever without written permission except in the case of brief quotations embodied in critical articles and reviews. For information address HarperCollins Children's Books, a division of HarperCollins Publishers, 195 Broadway, New York, NY 10007. www.icanread.com

Library of Congress Control Number: 2016936323
ISBN 978-0-06-235029-9 (trade bdg.) — ISBN 978-0-06-235028-2 (pbk.)

18 19 20 LSCC 10 9 8 7 6 5

❖

First Edition

The Berenstain Bears®

We Love Baseball!

Mike Berenstain

Based on the characters created by
Stan and Jan Berenstain

HARPER
An Imprint of HarperCollins*Publishers*

Grizzly Gramps loves baseball.

His favorite team is the Bear

Town Badgers.

"There's a big game today!"

says Gramps.

"Let's all go down to the ballpark."

The rest of the family

likes baseball, too.

They put on their Badgers caps.

They put on their Badgers shirts.

They are ready for the game.

The parking lot is full.

The crowd goes through the gates.

They get their tickets punched.

The cubs get bobblehead dolls.

"Look!" said Sister. "It's Babe Bear!"

The family finds their seats.

They look out over the green field.

It's a nice day for baseball.

The Badgers are warming up.
"There's the *real* Babe Bear!"
says Brother Bear.

The other team warms up, too.
They are the Grizzly Growlers.
They look pretty good.

The Badgers' mascot is in a badger suit.

He does the Badger Dance.

He turns a flip.

He's funny! Everyone laughs.

A loudspeaker says,
"And now our Bear Country
Anthem."
All take off their hats.

They all sing,
"'Our country, 'tis of thee,
Sweet land of li-bear-ty,
Of thee I sing!'"

When the anthem is over,

everyone cheers.

“Play ball!” says the umpire.

The first batter is up.

"Papa," says Honey.

She whispers in his ear.

"Oh," says Papa. "Come along."

Papa takes Honey to the restroom.

He hears cheering.

It’s a big play.

He misses it!

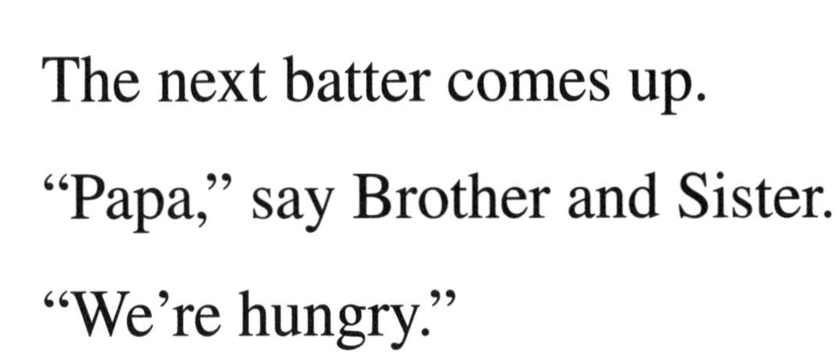

The next batter comes up.
"Papa," say Brother and Sister.
"We're hungry."

Papa takes the cubs for food.

He hears cheering.

It's another big play.

He misses it!

Papa and the cubs

go back to their seats.

The next batter comes up.

He hits a foul ball.

"I got it! I got it!" says Papa.

He misses it.

But Honey catches it.

Everyone cheers.

The Badgers' mascot is getting tired.

He takes off his head.

He needs a rest.

"Let me have a turn!" says Papa.

He puts on the badger suit.

Papa dances the Badger Dance.

He does a flip.

He slips and does an even bigger flip.

He's funny! Everyone laughs.

Now it’s time to stretch.

Everyone starts to sing,

“‘Take me out to the ball game.

Take me out with the crowd.

Buy me some peanuts

and Cracker Jack.

I don’t care if I never get back!’”

There's a close play at home plate.

"You're out!" says the ump.

"He's safe!" yells Grizzly Gramps.

"Now, Gramps," says Grizzly Gran.

"But he was safe!" says Gramps.

"Just calm down," says Gran.

"Yes, dear," says Gramps.

The game is tied up.

It's almost over.

Babe Bear comes up to bat.

He points to the fence.

The ball comes in. Babe Bear swings.

The ball flies over the fence.

It's a home run!

The Badgers win!

The game is over.

The crowd leaves the park.

The cubs wiggle their bobblehead dolls.

Honey swings her doll's little bat around.

"Home run!" says Gramps.

"Yay!" they all cry. "Go Badgers!"

Papa does the Badger Dance—

but not the flip!